This book belongs to

_____

DAISY'S NATURE HUNT

Disney's

READ *and* GROW LIBRARY

Published by Advance Publishers
Winter Park, Florida

Written by Janet Craig   Edited by Bonnie Brook
Penciled by Carlo Lo Raso   Painted by Stacia Martin
Designed by Design Five
Cover art by Peter Emslie
Cover design by Irene Yap

ISBN: 1-885222-87-4
10 9 8 7 6 5 4 3 2 1

It was a beautiful spring day! Huey, Dewey, and Louie rushed outside to play.

"How about helping me set up this hammock?" said Donald. "Today seems like a good day for a nap."

"Sure, Unca Donald," answered Louie. Soon the ends of the hammock were tied to two tall trees.

Donald was just about to lie down,
when Daisy rode up on her bicycle.

"Hi, boys," she said. "Would you like to
go on a nature hunt?"

"Wow!" said Dewey. "That sounds like
fun! Want to help us, Unca Donald?"

"Aw, phooey!" Donald said to himself.
He wanted to take a nap.

But out loud, he said, "Ah…I don't know, boys. I think I might be coming down with a fever. Maybe I should lie down in the hammock for a little while."

"Okay," said the boys. "We'll see you later."

"I hope Unca Donald's all right," said Louie.

"I think the only fever Donald has is spring fever!" said Daisy, laughing. "But I'll go check on him just in case while you boys start the nature hunt. I'll tell you where to find the first clue—it's on the big oak tree."

Huey, Dewey, and Louie ran to the oak. Tacked to its bark was a mysterious-looking note. It said:

Follow the clues, one by one.
If you do, you'll have some fun.
Your search will bring you lots of pleasure
And, in the end, a special treasure!

"A treasure!" said Dewey. "What could it be?"

"Let's find out," said Huey. "I see another clue."

The boys dashed across the yard and found the clue hidden near a small plant.

If you dig, you'll find below
The seed from which an oak
will grow.

Gently, the boys used their hands to dig up the plant.

"Look," said Huey. "It's an acorn!"

"Remember how the squirrels buried acorns last fall?" asked Louie. "They were saving them for food."

"It looks as if they forgot to dig up this acorn," said Dewey. "Now it's growing into an oak tree."

The boys carefully replanted the tiny tree, so that it could grow into a big, strong tree some day.

The next clue lay hidden among the tulips:

Listen closely and you'll hear
Our chirping—it is loud and clear.

Huey, Dewey, and Louie listened very carefully. Soon they heard the chirping of baby birds! They followed the sounds to a bird nest, where they saw a mother bird feed her babies a worm which she had pulled from the ground.

A little brown sparrow flew back and forth, carrying straw and twigs to make its nest.

A tiny hummingbird hovered by a flower. It was collecting sweet nectar with its long beak and tongue.

"I wonder where our next clue is," said Louie.

"Maybe we should check on Unca Donald first," said Dewey.

They ran over to Donald in his hammock.

"How are you feeling, Unca Donald?" asked Huey.

"Perfect, boys," said Donald. "Just perfect."

"Then are you ready to help us?" said Louie.

Suddenly Donald remembered he was supposed to be sick.

"Phooey," Donald thought as he started to get out of the hammock. "Oh," he said aloud, "I think I just hurt my back. Maybe I should rest a little bit more."

The boys had just helped Donald back into his hammock when they found another clue:

I'm a tree that blooms in May.
My fruit helps keep the doctor away.

"I know what it is!" said Huey. "It's the apple tree." Huey, Dewey, and Louie ran over to the tree. It was covered with lovely pink and white flowers.

"Just think," said Huey. "In the fall, instead of flowers, this tree will be covered with apples. Yum!"

"Gosh, just thinking about those apples makes me hungry," said Louie.

"Me, too," agreed Huey and Dewey.

Just then Daisy arrived with a plate of cookies.

"I thought you might want a snack," she said.

"You were right!" said Louie.

The boys sat down beneath the tree to eat their cookies. Before long, they noticed several ants crawling past. Each one, small as it was, picked up a big cookie crumb and carried it away.

"Wow," said Huey. "Ants are strong for their size."

"Our Junior Woodchuck guide says that ants work in colonies," said Dewey.

"Each one has a job," said Louie.

"Some ants, like these, are workers," said Huey, watching the ants crawl into an anthill. "They carry food back down that hole for the other ants."

As the boys and Daisy watched the ants, they noticed another small creature scurrying through the grass.

"Is that an ant, too?" asked Louie.

"It's a spider," said Daisy. "It looks a little bit like an ant, but it has eight legs instead of six."

As he watched the spider disappear into the grass, Louie saw some thin silken strands woven together in a detailed pattern. It was the spider's web.

"Some spiders can be harmful to us," Daisy said, "but others help us by getting rid of harmful insects."

Daisy passed Donald on the way back to the house. He jumped out of the hammock to get a cookie.

"Your back must be feeling better," said Daisy. "Why don't you help the boys on their nature hunt?"

That sounded like work to Donald, so he quickly started limping.

"Darn," he said. "I must have twisted my ankle. I'm going to have to rest in the hammock a little longer."

Meanwhile, the boys were approaching the high grass in the backyard.

Suddenly, Dewey whispered, "Quiet, everyone—look!"

There was a little brown rabbit hidden in the grass.

At first the rabbit stayed very still, twitching only its nose and long ears. It was smelling for danger with its nose and listening carefully with its ears to be sure the boys didn't come any closer.

Suddenly, the rabbit sprang off, hopping away on its strong hind legs.

Huey, Dewey, and Louie knew from their Junior Woodchuck guide that the rabbit was trying to lead them away from its nest of babies, which was hidden in the tall grass nearby.

As they carefully tried to peek through the grass, the boys found another clue:

Some people tell me to "fly away home,"
But it's in your garden I'd rather roam.
I look for a meal that's a tasty treat.
Bad bugs and insects are what I eat!

"I know what it is!" said Huey. "It's a ladybug!" He reached down into the grass and carefully scooped one up. It had a red shell sprinkled with black spots.

"Did you know that gardeners like ladybugs?" said Dewey. "That's because ladybugs eat lots of the bugs that harm their garden plants."

Huey lifted his hand, and the ladybug flew off.
Then the boys found their next clue:

I wear a brown-and-white striped suit,
And stuff my cheeks with nuts and fruit.

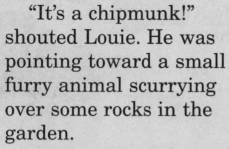

"It's a chipmunk!" shouted Louie. He was pointing toward a small furry animal scurrying over some rocks in the garden.

The chipmunk was looking for fruit, nuts, and seeds.

"I know what he's doing," said Huey.

"He's gathering food for winter," said Dewey.

"He stores it in his underground burrow," said Louie. "Then, in the winter, he can sleep and eat down there where it's warm."

"That reminds me of Unca Donald," Dewey laughed.

As Dewey raced to the edge of the yard trying to find the next clue, Huey cried out.

"Look out, Dewey!" he said. "You're headed straight into poison ivy!"

Dewey stopped short. He remembered how itchy the poison ivy leaves had made him last summer.

"How did you know it was poison ivy?" Dewey asked as the boys ran back into the yard.

"That's easy," said Huey. "Just look for a climbing plant with shiny green leaves growing in groups of three. Then stay away!"

Soon the boys found another clue taped
to a rock:

> *You've followed the clues, one by one.*
> *You've seen so much and had some fun!*
> *Now go back to the old oak tree.*
> *A treasure awaits—what can it be?*

The boys raced back to the old oak
tree, excited to find their treasure.

But when they got there, all they saw was the tree itself. They ran over to Uncle Donald who was still lazily swinging in his hammock.

"Have you seen our treasure?" asked Huey.

"A treasure?" said Donald, yawning and stretching. "There's no treasure here."

Sadly, the boys retreated
to a shady spot under the tree.

"Aunt Daisy wouldn't have
fooled us," said Huey.

"Naw, she's too nice," said
Dewey.

"Do you think she forgot?"
asked Louie.

Just then, Daisy strolled up.

"Oh, there you are, boys," said Daisy. "Would you mind helping me carry this big trunk out of the garage?"

A little while later, Huey, Dewey, and Louie were dragging the big trunk across the lawn.

"Thanks, boys," said Daisy. "Now will you help me open it?"

Inside, there was a big note:

Congratulations. You've finished your quest.
This trunk is really your treasure chest.

"You didn't forget us!" cried Huey.

"Of course not," Daisy replied, smiling.

"Look!" cried Dewey, looking in the trunk. "There are hoes, shovels, rakes, seeds,…everything we need to make a garden!"

Donald sprang up. Helping the boys make a garden— now that sounded like fun!

"Want some help, boys?" he said.

Daisy winked at the boys. Then she pulled a straw hat from the trunk and plunked it on Donald's head. "Perhaps you'd like a job that doesn't require much energy," she said with a giggle.

"Yes, you can be our scarecrow!" said the boys.

Everybody laughed, even Donald. Then, together, they began to plant their garden.